A Friend for
Bently

Written and illustrated by

Paige Keiser

HARPER

An Imprint of HarperCollins*Publishers*

ISBN 978-0-06-264332-2

The artist used Winsor and Newton watercolors and
colored pencil to create the illustrations for this book.

Typography by Rachel Zegar

19   20   21   22   23   SCP   10   9   8   7   6   5   4   3   2   1

❖

First Edition

For Mom and Dad,
whose unending love and support
led me to the creation of this book

Bently was the only pig on Sunset Farm.

—tra-la...

He had no one to play in the mud with. The sheep found it too dirty for their clean white wool.

He had no one to eat slop with. The chickens preferred seeds and worms.

He also had no one to do the crossword puzzle with,
because the goats preferred eating the pages.

One day Bently sat alone in the meadow and leaned his head back. "Oink!" he called out.

Oink!—

Suddenly someone oinked back! His little heart
thumped with joy in his chest. Another pig!

Bently followed the *oink*s
until he found a small dirt pile.
There, dusting herself in the
dirt, was a chick named Daisy.

"Have you seen a pig around here?" he asked the chick.

"No, sorry," said Daisy.

Bently sat down and heaved a long sigh.

Maybe it was all in his imagination?

"Why so glum?" asked Daisy.

"I thought I heard another pig oinking over this way."

"Do I really sound like an actual pig?" she asked excitedly.

"What?" asked Bently.

"I was born a chicken, but I'd much rather be a pig. They have way more fun. All chickens do is sit around and lay eggs. And I hate worms!"

Bently was quite surprised.

"That was *you* oinking?" he finally said.

"I'm practicing rolling in the dirt—see?" said Daisy.
"When I get good enough, I can move on to mud!"
"I can teach you that," said Bently. "Hop on."

Bently was still a little disappointed, but he soon got over it as he began teaching Daisy the ways of the pig.

Bently shared his slop with Daisy, who found it so much tastier than seeds and worms.

Bently was also surprised that Daisy was a whiz
at crossword puzzles!

Daisy was yellow instead of pink, and several
pounds lighter than the average pig, but she made
Bently very happy with her friendship.

Oink!

By the time fall arrived, Daisy had become a full-grown chicken. But things began to change.

She started to prefer the dry dust to the dirty mud.

She began to prefer seeds and worms to slop.

And crosswords no longer
interested her.

zzz...Cluck...zzz

zzz...DAISY...zzz...

Even though Daisy's interests had changed, she still cared deeply for Bently.

So Daisy entered a crossword puzzle contest run by another local farm, and she won! The prize was . . .

...A PIG!

Bently couldn't believe his eyes when he saw the new pig. His heart thumped with joy once again, and they became fast friends.

Daisy was glad to see Bently happy again.

And once in a while, when the full moon appeared over the trees, Daisy would join Bently and his new friend, Morgan, for an all-night crossword puzzle marathon.

zzzOinkOinkCluck!zzz...